PRESENTS

THE AMERICAN GIRLS COLLECTION

1854

MEET KIRSTEN · An American Girl
KIRSTEN LEARNS A LESSON · A School Story
KIRSTEN'S SURPRISE · A Christmas Story
HAPPY BIRTHDAY, KIRSTEN! · A Springtime Story
KIRSTEN SAVES THE DAY · A Summer Story
CHANGES FOR KIRSTEN · A Winter Story

1904

MEET SAMANTHA · An American Girl
SAMANTHA LEARNS A LESSON · A School Story
SAMANTHA'S SURPRISE · A Christmas Story
HAPPY BIRTHDAY, SAMANTHA! · A Springtime Story
SAMANTHA SAVES THE DAY · A Summer Story
CHANGES FOR SAMANTHA · A Winter Story

1944

MEET MOLLY · An American Girl
MOLLY LEARNS A LESSON · A School Story
MOLLY'S SURPRISE · A Christmas Story
HAPPY BIRTHDAY, MOLLY! · A Springtime Story
MOLLY SAVES THE DAY · A Summer Story
CHANGES FOR MOLLY · A Winter Story

Changes for Kirsten

A Winter Story

By Janet Shaw

Illustrations Renée Graef

Vignettes Keith Skeen

Pleasant Company

For information address Pleasant Company, 7 North Pinckney Street, Madison, Wisconsin 53703.
Printed in the United States of America
First Edition.

PICTURE CREDITS

The following individuals and organizations have generously given permission to reprint illustrations contained in "Looking Back:" pp. 60-61—S. Holmes Andrews, Minnesota Historical Society; Early Settler Life Series, Crabtree Publishing Company, New York; Early Settler Life Series, Crabtree Publishing Company, New York; pp. 62-63—State Historical Society of Wisconsin; State Historical Society of Wisconsin; State Historical Society of Wisconsin; pp. 64-65—State Historical Society of Wisconsin; As seen in *Pioneer America,* by Carl Drepperd, published by Doubleday; As seen in *Pioneer America,* by Carl Drepperd, published by Doubleday; State Historical Society of Wisconsin; Philadelphia Museum of Art: The Edgar William and Bernice Chrysler Garbisch Collection.

Edited by Jeanne Thieme
Designed by Myland McRevey
Art Directed by Kathleen A. Brown

Library of Congress Cataloging-in-Publication Data

Shaw, Janet Beeler, 1937-
Changes for Kirsten: a winter story

by Janet Shaw; illustrations, Renée Graef; vignettes, Keith Skeen.
p. cm.—(The American girls collection)
Summary: A tough Minnesota winter brings many changes to Kirsten's frontier life, including the new responsibilty of helping her brother Lars set his traps and a move into a new house for her family.
ISBN 0-937295-44-2 ISBN 0-937295-45-0 (pbk.)
[1. Frontier and pioneer life—Fiction. 2. Minnesota—Fiction.]
I. Graef, Renée, ill. II. Title. III. Series.
PZ7.S53423Ch 1988 [Fic]—dc19 88-19578 CIP AC

FOR MY MOTHER,
NADINA FOWLER

Table of Contents

KIRSTEN
A ten-year-old who moves with her family to a new home on America's frontier in 1854.

PAPA, LARS, MAMA, PETER, AND BABY BRITTA
The Larsons sometimes long for Sweden, but they never lose heart for the challenges of pioneer life.

SINGING BIRD
Kirsten's secret friend, an Indian girl.

MISS WINSTON
Kirsten's teacher, who lived with Uncle Olav's family.

ANNA, AUNT INGER, LISBETH, AND UNCLE OLAV
Kirsten's American relatives live on a new farm in Minnesota, where they make the Larson family feel at home.

CHAPTER
ONE

ON THE TRAP LINE

"Kirsten can't come with us!" John Stewart said. "Trapping is work for boys, not girls."

"Let her come along," Kirsten's brother Lars said. "Kirsten knows the forest. She knows the ways of the animals. She can help us out, John."

But John crossed his arms over his chest and shook his head. "Setting traps is dangerous. She could get hurt."

"She won't set traps," Lars said. "She'll help us decide *where* to set traps."

"Opening the traps and taking the animals out is dangerous, too!" John spoke as though Kirsten weren't standing right next to him.

"You and I will open the traps and get the animals out. After we skin them, Kirsten can help carry the pelts home," Lars said. "Just yesterday you said we should bring someone along to help us."

"And today I say she stays home with the women and children!" John said. "Trapping is hard enough without a girl to look after."

Kirsten bit her lip and looked down at her boots. The January snow came up almost to her knees. She wore all her flannel petticoats, her warmest skirt, and two pairs of wool socks, but still she trembled with cold. Her breath was a frost on her muffler. It would get colder yet as the afternoon went on. Winter in Minnesota was much harder than the winters in Sweden! But Kirsten wanted to go with Lars and John on the trap line. She was tired of working in the small, smoky cabin. And Lars was right—she did know about animals and the forest. She could help on the trap line, if only John would give her a chance.

"She knows how to spot the holes where beavers come through the ice," Lars said. "She knows the tracks raccoons make, and the tracks of muskrats and foxes. She can help us choose where to set traps for them. Don't be stubborn, John."

John peered down at Kirsten and frowned. "What will you do if we find a live beaver in a trap? It might bite you!"

"If we find a live beaver, I'll stay back," Kirsten said firmly. "Don't worry, I won't get bitten."

"Let her come with us this once," Lars said.

John huffed out a white breath. "All right. She can come this one time. But if she's trouble, she can't come again. Agreed, Kirsten?"

Kirsten looked him right in the eye. "Agreed," she said.

"Then let's go!" Lars said. "It's already afternoon, and we have a long, long way to walk before dark."

He swung his arms to get the warmth back into his hands, then strapped on his snowshoes. John and Kirsten strapped on snowshoes, too, and pulled their rucksacks onto their backs.

John was thirteen, but almost as tall as Lars. He had cheerful brown eyes and curly dark hair like his sister Mary. Mary was Kirsten's friend. Why wouldn't John be friends, too? Why was he so set against Kirsten going along on the trap line?

Lars picked up the rifle and followed John into the woods. Kirsten hugged herself for warmth, but she kept up with the boys' long strides.

They were going to check each of the traps the boys had set in the woods. If it was a good day, they would find dead animals in many of the traps. They'd skin the animals, dry the fur pelts, and sell the pelts at the general store.

The boys did this hard work because Papa, Uncle Olav, and John's father were gone for the winter. The men were working in a logging camp where they could make money cutting down trees. In the spring they would come back home. Until then, the women and children had to do all the winter farm work and make what money they could. Kirsten thought it was awful to have Papa gone. But she knew there was no other way her family could save money for a farm of their own.

As Kirsten walked, she studied the deer tracks that crossed the trail. She watched a red-tailed hawk circling overhead. She spied the bright red swoop of a cardinal. She was so happy to be out of the cabin and into the woods that she forgot how cold it was or how far she had walked with Lars and John.

They were in deep woods, far from the cabin, when Kirsten saw something strange—a birch tree bent over by a length of rope staked to the ground. "Lars, John, look!" she said.

The boys stopped. John didn't seem surprised to see the bent tree and the rope. "That's a snare trap for mink," he said.

"A trap made with rope?" Kirsten said. "All our traps are metal."

"We set metal traps because they're modern," John said. "But Old Jack still traps the old-fashioned way, with rope traps. That trap must be one of his."

"Who's Old Jack?" Kirsten asked.

John stamped back to the trail, and Kirsten hurried to keep up with him.

"Old Jack is the oldest trapper in these parts," John told her. "He came west as an explorer and stayed on. He lives by himself, way back in the woods. He doesn't have a family and never did."

"Old Jack dresses all in leather clothes, the

"That must be one of Old Jack's traps," John said.
"Old Jack still traps the old-fashioned way."

old way,'' Lars added.

''Ohhhh,'' Kirsten said.

John grinned over his shoulder at her. ''There's nothing to be scared of. Old Jack is different, but he's wise. Once he showed me where to set some traps for foxes. He likes to trap mink and martens and fishers—furs worth a lot of money.''

''Well, I hope we don't meet up with Old Jack,'' Kirsten said. She peered into the purple shadows under the pines.

''If we did meet Old Jack, he'd give us a hand,'' John said. ''But I doubt if we'll see him. He doesn't like to come where other folks are.''

As John spoke, Kirsten saw a big jack rabbit jump from under a pine tree. Quickly, she pointed. Lars had the rifle at his shoulder. He took a shot, and the rabbit tumbled down. ''Rabbit stew for supper tonight!'' Lars said. He ran ahead to pick up the rabbit.

Kirsten thought of the delicious stew Mama made with carrots and onions and potatoes. Her stomach moaned with hunger, and she munched a piece of bread from her pocket. It would be a long time before they would be home for supper.

"Our traps begin in that ravine," Lars said. "Come on!"

In the first trap, they found a big raccoon. Lars quickly skinned it and put the skin in his rucksack.

In the second trap they found another. "We're having good luck today," John said as he skinned the raccoon.

"Maybe it's because Kirsten came along," Lars said. He winked at her.

"Maybe it's because we set our traps right," John said in his stubborn way. But Kirsten thought he almost smiled at her.

She tucked her hands under her armpits for warmth and looked up the hill into the oak trees. The sun was sinking low behind them. Many animals in the forest slept all day and woke up at dusk. At this time of day she might see a deer, Kirsten thought.

And as though she'd wished it here, a big buck stepped into the clearing! He appeared as silently as a shadow. Kirsten held her breath. Her heart was beating fast. The buck was so beautiful. But before Lars could reach for his rifle, the buck leaped away.

They saw his white tail flash, and he was gone. Lars slapped his knee in disappointment. "If I'd shot him, there would have been meat for our family and yours, too, John!"

"We've got the rabbit," John said. "And we might find some muskrats in the water traps. They're good to eat, too. Let's go on."

It wasn't long before John, Lars, and Kirsten each had a rucksack full of pelts. It was growing dark when they came to the last trap. A small raccoon was in it. When Lars bent down to spring the trap, the raccoon opened its bright eyes and raised a paw.

"Look, just its tail is caught," John said. "It's not even bloody. I think the trap only bumped its head and knocked it out."

The young raccoon pawed at Lars' mitten but didn't even show its teeth.

"It's dazed, that's all," Lars said. "Anyway, it's too little to be worth anything. Let's let it go."

Kirsten knelt to look at the young raccoon. It made a noise like a kitten. Its pawprints in the snow looked like little hands. She knew a stunned raccoon wouldn't live long in the woods. A wolverine

or a badger would get it. "Let me take it home," she said. "I can take care of it until it gets strong enough to look after itself. Then I'll let it go."

Lars shook his head as though he couldn't believe his ears. "You can't make a pet out of a wild animal, Kirsten!"

"I won't make a pet of it. I'll just keep it until it's healthy again," Kirsten said. "Remember how I nursed the crow with the broken wing?"

"That was a bird," Lars said. "Raccoons are different. You know how much trouble they cause at the farm."

The little raccoon pawed at the tip of her snowshoe. It *was* almost like a kitten, Kirsten thought. If she kept it in a box for a few days, it would be strong again.

John bent down and picked up the raccoon. It still didn't show its teeth. "I don't understand why it's so gentle," he said.

"It won't be gentle when it comes to its senses," Lars said. "Let it go, John."

But instead of letting the raccoon go, John handed it to Kirsten. "You do seem to know about animals, Kirsten. Maybe you can help this one."

His smile told her he was glad she'd come trapping with them. Although her lips were numb with cold, she smiled back at him.

She put the raccoon into her rucksack on top of the furs. "Come on, the moon is up already," she said. "Let's hurry home before we get caught in the dark." She wrapped her muffler over her nose and went ahead of the boys down the trail toward the little farm in the valley.

Chapter Two

Fire!

After supper, Lars and John divided the pelts into two equal piles. John took his share home. Lars and Kirsten took theirs to the barn. Kirsten found an empty nail box, lined it with hay, and put the little raccoon inside. It nestled down and closed its eyes. Then Kirsten and Lars pulled the pelts over wooden stretchers and scraped them with knives.

As she scraped the pelts, Kirsten watched the raccoon sleep. It seemed tame already. She thought there was no need to worry about it causing trouble.

Soon Mama came to the barn to call them for bed. Her eyes went wide when she saw the raccoon in the box. "Children, why did you bring a raccoon home? You know how much mischief they cause!" she said. "Remember the raccoon that stole the fish for our supper right off the table?"

Lars looked up from his work. "This raccoon was knocked out by a trap. Kirsten brought it home so it can get on its feet again."

"Wild animals don't want to be touched," Mama said. "If it let you pick it up, maybe it's sick. Sick animals can be dangerous."

Kirsten covered the raccoon's box with a piece of wood. "It's not sick, Mama. It's just dazed and needs rest. When it's stronger, I'll let it go," she said softly. She thought of John's smile when he put the little raccoon into her hands—John wanted to be her friend.

Mama pulled her thick shawl over her head. Even in the barn it was shivering cold tonight. "I don't think your papa would want a wild animal in the barn. Be sure you keep it in the box, Kirsten."

Lars picked up the lantern and put his hand on Mama's shoulder. "Let's go back to the cabin, Mama. And don't worry. It's just a little raccoon. Kirsten will take care of it."

Mama sighed. "But you mustn't bring it near the cabin. And let it go the minute it seems well, do you promise?"

"I promise," Kirsten said quickly. She thought her mother looked very tired. Mama had so much work to do these days, and she missed Papa. They all missed Papa.

Before they left the barn, Kirsten put the raccoon's box under the hay where it was warmer. "Get well," she whispered to the sleeping raccoon. "Get well quickly!"

❤

When Kirsten woke up the next morning, the first thing she thought of was the raccoon. But there wasn't time for her to go look at it. She had to feed baby Britta her oatmeal. And she had to make breakfast for everyone. Today was baking day, and Mama was already busy making dough for their bread.

"Kirsten, I'm going up to Aunt Inger's house to bake our bread in her big oven," Mama said. She picked up the tray of dough. "While I'm gone, I want you to wash out the diapers and help Peter learn his numbers and—"

"And look after Britta!" Kirsten finished for Mama.

Mama smiled. "That baby sister of yours does need a lot of looking after, doesn't she?"

"She crawls everywhere!" Peter said.

Britta pulled herself up on his knee and tugged at the slate he held. In her long flannel dress and many sweaters, Britta was as chubby as a bear cub. She *was* sweet, but she was a lot of trouble, too.

Peter raised the slate out of her reach. "I wish it wasn't too cold to have school," he said.

"I've never heard you wish for school before," Mama said.

"Britta can't come to school." Peter scowled.

Mama rumpled his yellow hair with her free hand. "I know it's hard to be cooped up in the cabin all winter. But soon it will be spring, and you'll be running outside again. While I'm gone you must shell the walnuts, Peter. When I come back, I'll make a little cake for supper. Be good children."

"Yes, Mama," Kirsten said as Mama went out the door. Kirsten wished she could go to Aunt Inger's house and play with her cousins Anna and

Lisbeth. She wished she could go on the trap line again today with Lars and John. But Mama needed her to stay in the cabin and work.

Kirsten chipped ice off the window and gazed at the barn. Was the little raccoon getting better? Was it warm enough in the box? Maybe she'd just take a quick peek at it before she did the washing.

"Peter, you hold Britta for a minute, will you? I'm going to run to the barn. When I get back, I'll tell you why."

Peter looked grumpy, but he held out his arms for the baby.

Without buttoning her sweater, Kirsten raced to the barn. She dug the raccoon's box out from under the hay and peeked under the board. Good! The raccoon's eyes were open. But the little thing trembled with cold. It missed its warm nest with the other raccoons. Kirsten decided that if she took the box to the cabin—just for a little while—the raccoon would warm up and get stronger more quickly. She tucked the box under her arm and ran back.

Kirsten set the box by the cookstove. "Come look, Peter!"

Peter put the baby down in the center of the bed and crouched beside Kirsten. She lifted the board. Peter peered in. "Kirsten, what a funny face it has! It looks so friendly!"

Before Kirsten could warn him not to, Peter scooped up the raccoon like a toy and set it on the floor.

Right away the raccoon dashed under the bed. "Catch it, Peter!" Kirsten said. Peter flopped onto his belly and grabbed for the scampering raccoon. But the frightened animal was much too quick for him. It darted across the floor under a chair.

"We have to catch it!" Kirsten snatched at the raccoon's striped tail. "It might break something!"

The raccoon raced up the chair and leaped onto the shelf by the cookstove. As it scurried across the shelf, it knocked a tin cup and a candlestick onto the floor.

Britta laughed out loud. She thought the chase was a new game. But Kirsten was alarmed. "Peter, get it back in the box!" she cried. Her fingers brushed the raccoon's paw. She almost had it!

Kirsten knew the raccoon wanted to get out of the cabin and back to the woods. Maybe she should open the door and let it run free. But before she could get to the door, the raccoon jumped on top of the table. Peter reached with both hands. The raccoon leaped and tipped over the oil lamp that sat on the table.

The lamp crashed to the floor and broke. Flames shot up from the spilled oil and caught the tablecloth.

"Oh, no! Oh, no!" Kirsten cried. She jerked the burning cloth from the table and stamped on it. But now the spilled oil spread. Suddenly the oil was a trail of fire across the floor!

How could she put out the fire? She dumped the wash water onto it, but that wasn't enough. The burning oil crept under the bed where Britta sat.

Kirsten grabbed the baby and pushed her into Peter's arms. "Run to Aunt Inger's, Peter! Tell everyone to come help! Tell them to bring water!"

She opened the door and shoved Peter on his way. The raccoon darted out right by his heels. "Hurry, Peter, hurry!" she called after him.

"Run to Aunt Inger's, Peter!" Kirsten cried.
"Tell everyone to come help! Tell them to bring water!"

Kirsten grabbed the coffeepot and splashed it on the fire under the bed, but that didn't help either. If only she had more water, a lot of water! Already flames had caught the blanket and the straw mattress. She beat at them with a rug. But quickly the fire spread up the cabin wall where the clothes hung. Moment by moment the fire grew stronger. Their cabin was burning down! What could she save?

She picked up the candlesticks Mama had brought from Sweden. Would Mama want her candlesticks most of all? Maybe the rifle was more important, or the stew pot. There wasn't time to think! Kirsten's eye caught the big blue trunk that had once held everything her family owned in America. The family Bible and their extra clothes were stored in the trunk. Surely it was the most important thing of all to save. She shoved the rifle and the candlesticks into the trunk and latched the lid.

But the trunk was so heavy! Kirsten could hardly budge it, and now the flames were climbing into the rafters over her head. Somehow she dragged the trunk to the door. Then she got behind it and shoved. The fire crackled at her back. Flames roared in the shingle roof overhead! Hurry, hurry! She put her shoulder to the trunk and pushed again.

As the trunk went through the door, Mama and Aunt Inger came running. "Mama, help me!" Kirsten cried.

"Kirsten, come here!" Mama grabbed Kirsten's hand and pulled her away from the burning cabin. Aunt Inger yanked the trunk away, too. Now Lisbeth and Anna and Peter came with buckets of water. They tossed the water at the fire. "More water!" Aunt Inger cried. She filled her apron with snow and pitched it at the fire. Lisbeth and Anna filled their buckets with snow to toss on the flames. Peter and Kirsten scooped snow with their hands and threw it. But the flames only leaped higher.

Fire filled the cabin and burst out the window and the door. The cabin burned like a giant bonfire, sending sparks up into the cold air.

"It's too late!" Mama cried. "Get back, everyone! Get back! Don't get hurt!"

As they backed away, the cabin roof crashed down into the flames with a roar. All they could do was watch as what was left of their home went up in black smoke.

Aunt Inger hugged Mama, and Mama hugged Kirsten and Peter, and Anna and Lisbeth hugged each other.

Tears rolled down Mama's face. "We're all safe, that's the most important thing," she said softly. She pressed Peter and Kirsten against her. "You two are safe. The baby is safe. Kirsten even saved our trunk. But what will we ever do now?"

"You'll come live in our house with us!" Aunt Inger said. "It won't be so bad, you'll see. You can start over again. Don't cry, dears!"

But Kirsten couldn't stop crying. Their pillows were burning, and their blankets, and their sweaters, and even the diapers for Britta. Their spoons were burning, and their tin plates and mugs, and even the washtub and the mixing bowls. All they had left in the world were the clothes on their backs and the things in the trunk.

How could they possibly get along? How could they possibly start over? And what would Papa say when he heard that their home had burned to the ground? She buried her face in Mama's shawl and wept.

CHAPTER
THREE

GOOD NEWS?

"I like it *better* with everyone living here! It's cozy!" Anna said. She was setting out bowls for the potato soup Aunt Inger had made. "And it's much warmer with four of us in our bed, isn't it, Lisbeth?"

Lisbeth cut thick slices of bread to go with the soup. "It's warmer with Kirsten and Peter in our bed, but Peter kicks," she said.

"I do not kick!" Peter said. "Anyway, you talk in your sleep, Lisbeth! Last night you sat straight up and pulled the blankets off, and you didn't even know it! I wish I could sleep in a drawer, like Britta."

"I wish you'd sleep on the floor, like Lars!"

Lisbeth said.

"Stop it, children!" Aunt Inger said. "Don't fuss about what can't be helped. Here, come have some soup."

"Is there enough soup for John and Mary, too?" Lars said. "They're coming soon. John and I are going to set beaver traps today." Lars was rubbing musk oil on the traps to hide the smell of his hands. Animals wouldn't come near a trap that smelled of humans.

"Yes, there's enough soup to share with them," Aunt Inger said. "Thank goodness the vegetables in your root cellar didn't burn."

"I hope they bring some bowls!" Lisbeth said. "We only have enough bowls for the eight of us."

"They can have their soup from a cup. No one goes hungry in our home," Aunt Inger said. "Lisbeth, why are you in a bad mood today?"

"I can't help it," Lisbeth said. She rubbed her forehead as though a tight band pressed there. "I try to be cheerful, but I just can't be!"

Kirsten gave Lisbeth's shoulder a friendly nudge. It was very, very hard on everyone to be crammed together all day and all night. "I'm going

to set traps with Lars and John," Kirsten said. "So you'll have extra space at the table to play with your paper dolls."

Lisbeth tried to smile. "Thank you, Kirsten."

With a bang! bang! bang! someone knocked at the cabin door. Peter unlatched it and John burst in. His sister Mary was right on his heels. Their cheeks were red and their brown eyes glowed. Kirsten thought she'd never seen such big, happy smiles as theirs.

"Hello! We've got soup for you two," Lars said.

"And we've got news for you!" John said. He stamped snow off his boots and pulled off his mittens.

"What news do you have for us?" Mama said quickly. She bounced the baby on her knee to keep her quiet.

Mary pulled folded papers from her pocket. "Some mail came to Mr. Berkhoff's store! He sent it to our house because we're closer to town than you are. We got a letter from our father, and here are two letters for the Larsons!"

Aunt Inger put the soup ladle right back in the pot and took the letter Mary handed her. Mama gave the baby to Kirsten and took the other letter. Everyone, even John and Mary, crowded around the table to hear the news.

Aunt Inger's lips moved as she read the letter from Uncle Olav. "He's well," she said. "He's making good money. He misses us, of course!" She smiled at Lisbeth and Anna. "He says when the thaw comes in April, they'll float the logs downstream to the sawmills. Then he'll be heading home."

Mama spread her letter on the table and bent over it. After she'd read a few lines to herself she started reading out loud:

> "The logging is going well. I hope to make a hundred dollars this winter. With that money and the money from your pelts, we can buy more land to farm."

"A hundred dollars! That *is* good news!" Lars cried.

But Mama's eyes filled with tears. She covered Papa's letter with her hands. "Papa hasn't gotten *my* letter yet. He doesn't know our cabin burned down. Building another cabin will take every bit of the money he'll earn. There won't be enough for land of our own."

Anna's eyes filled with tears, too. When anyone cried, she always cried with them. "But we'll help you build a cabin!"

"I know you'll help us build," Mama said. She squeezed Anna's hand. "But starting over is so hard! When we came to America, we hoped to have a good house like the one we left behind in Sweden. Now we don't have even beds of our own."

Aunt Inger tossed her head as though shaking off all their troubles. "John, you said your family had good news. Tell us your good news!"

"Yes, tell them!" Mary said. She squeezed onto the bench beside Kirsten.

John jumped up off the trunk where he'd been sitting. "Listen to this! Father writes that he's going to be the manager of a logging camp! He'll run the whole camp. He'll be in charge of all the other men. And here's the best part—it's an Oregon camp!"

"Ore-gon camp?" Peter said. "What's Ore-gon?"

"Starting over is so hard!" Mama said.
"Now we don't have even beds of our own."

"*Where* is Oregon," Lisbeth corrected him. "Oregon is a place."

"Oregon's a place far, far west, beyond the prairie and even the mountains." John was so excited that he slapped his leg as he spoke. "There are big forests of redwood and spruce to cut in Oregon. It's fine logging country!"

"How will your father travel all that way west to Oregon?" Mama asked.

"In a covered wagon on the Oregon Trail," John said. "But it's not just Father who's going to Oregon! Our whole family will go west! We'll sell our house, and with the money we'll buy a wagon and oxen and everything we need. In the spring, when Father comes home, we'll join a wagon train and head west for Oregon!"

"The Oregon Trail!" Lars almost shouted. "I'd give anything to be going with you!"

Kirsten wanted to be happy for John and Mary and their family. But her spirits sank low. Mary was one of her closest friends. John was almost like another brother. When they left for Oregon, she would miss them very, very much.

"Everything's always changing," Kirsten said softly.

"I like things to change," Lars said. "I like things to be new!"

"Me, too!" John said. "And everything's new in Oregon!"

Everyone started talking at the same time. "We'll miss you!" "When will you leave?" "Are there schools in Oregon?" "Are there stores?"

Kirsten thought that everyone was excited and happy except her. She was half-happy and half-sad.

She slipped her arm around Mary's waist. "Mary, when you leave for Oregon, we might never see you again," Kirsten said. That was the sad part.

"We can write letters to each other," Mary said.

"Anyway, *I'll* see you again!" Lars said confidently. "I'll come out to Oregon as soon as I can!"

"We'll meet out there," John said. "Maybe we can lead wagon trains together, Lars!"

Then Aunt Inger clanked the soup ladle against the pot to get attention. "The Stewarts' move to Oregon is good for them and good for you, too," she said to Mama. "The Stewarts want to sell their house. Your house has burned, and you need a new one. You can buy the Stewarts' house. Then they'll have the money they need to move west, and you'll have the home you want. Isn't that wonderful?"

Mama folded Papa's letter and slipped it into her apron pocket. "It would be wonderful to buy the Stewarts' house if we had the money for it."

"How much will your house cost, John?" Aunt Inger said. She spread her hands on her hips the way she did when she bargained with Mr. Berkhoff at his store.

"Father told us to sell the house and furniture for five hundred dollars," John said.

Aunt Inger pursed her lips and frowned. Now she didn't look so happy. "Five hundred dollars for your house and furniture? Your house has four rooms and each one has a window. It has a good wooden floor and a shingle roof. Five hundred dollars is a fair price, all right. But it *is* a lot of money."

"Papa wrote he'll only make a hundred dollars cutting logs," Mama said softly.

"But don't forget we're going to sell the pelts

from our trap line," Lars said. "Then maybe we'll have enough money to buy the house."

"Even if you caught something in every trap every day, we still wouldn't have five hundred dollars," Mama said. "It's better not to hope to buy a house like the Stewarts'. It's better just to plan to build another little cabin like the one we had. That's all we can do." She sighed and took the baby back from Kirsten.

Aunt Inger sighed, too. "Come on, children, eat this good soup while it's hot. And you two, thank you for bringing us the letters. Let's hear some more about this place called Oregon."

CHAPTER FOUR

OLD JACK

"We could set these new beaver traps downstream," Kirsten said as she and Lars set out toward the stream a few days later. "I've seen beaver dams there. Near their dams is a good place to trap them."

"Good idea," Lars said. He pulled a big toboggan piled with the traps he'd prepared. "I say we give it a try."

"I say we do, too," Kirsten said. Her hands and feet tingled in the cold afternoon, but she wanted to be as hopeful and determined as Lars.

Today, John was checking the old trap line by himself so Lars and Kirsten could set traps for a new one. They were working extra hard because soon spring would come and the trapping season would be over. The Stewarts needed money for their move to Oregon. The Larsons needed a lot of money for a new home. So the children needed all the furs they could possibly trap, and there was no time to waste!

As Kirsten and Lars walked along the stream, Kirsten looked for trails of bubbles frozen in the ice. Beavers made the bubbles when they swam under the ice from their nests to shore. Each time Kirsten found a bubble trail, Lars dug a hole in the ice and lowered a trap into the water. The next time a beaver came this way, it would swim into their trap.

But there weren't as many bubble trails along this part of the stream as they'd hoped. When dusk came, they still had several traps left to set.

"We'll have to take these traps home with us," Lars said. "We can't stay out any longer. It will be dark soon."

"But look, Lars, here's a great spot!" Kirsten said. Right at her feet a trail of bubbles came to the bank. "Let's set just one more trap before we go back!"

Lars chopped a hole in the ice with his pick. Kirsten lowered the trap through the hole and into the water. As they turned back to their toboggan, an owl swooped low over their heads.

Lars peered after the owl and frowned. "Kirsten, if the owls are out, it's even later than I thought. We've got to hurry home."

The owl's hoot made Kirsten tremble. She'd heard stories about settlers who were caught in the woods at night. In this cold, she and Lars could freeze to death. Or a wolf might get them. "Let's run, Lars!" she said.

"It's hard to run in snowshoes," Lars said.

"Maybe we could take a short cut through the woods," Kirsten said. "That would be faster than following the stream. I think that if we follow the North Star, we'll find the farm. Come on, let's go!"

In a short time they were away from the stream and into the deep woods. Lars kept his eye on the North Star and led the way. But there was no trail to follow, and it was hard to pull the toboggan.

"It's going to be dark soon. I wish we had a lantern!" Kirsten said. Then she spotted snowshoe tracks in the snow. "Lars, look!" she cried. "Someone's made a trail here!"

Lars crouched down to study the tracks. "These look like they were made with old-fashioned snowshoes. I bet they're Old Jack's! John told me that Old Jack lived somewhere in this part of the woods. If this is Old Jack's trail, we're in luck!"

"Why?" Kirsten asked.

"Because we can follow the trail to where he lives, that's why," Lars said. "He'll lend us a lantern, I'm sure of it."

"Old Jack sounds spooky to me," Kirsten said. "I'm scared of him."

"Are you more scared of Old Jack or of losing our way in the woods?" Lars said.

Again the owl hooted, and now there were faint howls that might be coyotes. Or wolves. Kirsten hugged herself. "I'm more scared of losing our way," she said in a very small voice.

"Then let's follow these tracks and see if we can find Old Jack's," Lars said. He took the lead as they turned onto the snowshoe trail.

The trail led them into a ravine. As they

followed the trail, the ravine got more and more narrow. Rocky bluffs rose on both sides, like walls. There was no room for a cabin here.

Then Kirsten spotted a rough plank set into the rocks. It almost looked like a door. Firewood was stacked by it. She pointed. "Look," she said. "There's a door. There must be a cave behind it. Someone has made a home in a cave."

"This has got to be Old Jack's!" Lars said.

"But Old Jack's not here," Kirsten said. "Look, there's no smoke coming out of his chimney."

"Even if he's not here, we can borrow a lantern," Lars said.

If Old Jack wasn't in the cave she didn't have to be scared, Kirsten thought. She followed Lars.

Drifted snow piled against the door. It didn't look like anyone had been through that door for several days. Lars knocked. No one answered. He rattled the latch.

"The door's unlatched," Lars said. He shoved at the boards with both hands, but the door didn't give. "Come on, Kirsten, help me get this door open."

Kirsten ducked under Lars' arms and put her shoulder against the planks.

"One, two, three, push!" Lars said. They both shoved as hard as they could. The door creaked and then suddenly swung in. Kirsten was pushing so hard she fell onto her knees inside the cave. Lars tumbled in against her.

For a moment she couldn't see anything at all. And then, right there in front of her, she made out a man sitting against the rocky wall! He was dressed in leather. And he was looking right at them!

At first Kirsten couldn't get her breath. Then she screamed. She scrambled to her feet and started to run. Lars grabbed her shoulders.

"Kirsten! Don't run! He won't hurt us."

"He *will* hurt us!" Kirsten cried.

Lars shook her to make her be still. "Kirsten! He *can't* hurt us. He couldn't hurt anyone, even if he wanted to. Old Jack's dead."

Kirsten peeked around Lars at the man sitting stiffly on the floor. His face was white. There was no cloud of breath at his lips. His eyes were glazed over. Lars was right—the man was dead.

"Oh, Lars! What will we do now?" Kirsten whispered.

Lars took a deep breath. "We'll find his flint and light a lantern. Then we'll think what to do."

Lars found the lantern, and Kirsten found the flint stone by the fire hole. She struck the flint stone until sparks set fire to a bit of hay. Then Lars lit the wick of the lantern. In the flickering light they could see Old Jack better. He was an old man with a white beard and rough hands. His pants and jacket were deerskin. He made Kirsten think of an animal of the forest—a fox, maybe.

"Poor Old Jack!" she said.

Lars pulled Old Jack's fur cap down over the dead man's eyes. "Rest in peace, Old Jack," he said.

"Rest in peace," Kirsten repeated after Lars.

"How do you think Old Jack could have died?" Kirsten asked.

"He was an old, old man," Lars said slowly. "He probably sat down to rest and his heart stopped beating. After a while the fire burned out, and his body froze."

Kirsten couldn't stop trembling. "Let's take the lantern and go home. Let's get away from here!"

"We're much, much safer in this cave than we are in the woods," Lars said. "Let's look around."

Kirsten was frightened, but Lars seemed sure of himself. She stayed by his side as he found a tin cup, an iron pot, a skinning knife, a few stretcher boards with mink and marten pelts on them. Then Lars lifted the lantern high so they could see into the back of the cave.

At first all Kirsten saw were some Indian blankets on a pile of straw. Then she made out a stack of furs piled all the way up to the roof of the cave.

Lars drew in a sharp breath. "Look at that, Kirsten! Look at all those pelts! Old Jack's trapped twice as many pelts as we have, and all of them the finest fur!" He stroked one of the mink pelts. "He was the best trapper around here, that's for sure. There aren't any more like him!"

Kirsten looked down at Old Jack's body. "John said Old Jack doesn't have any family at all."

"No, he was alone in the world," Lars said.

"What will happen to Old Jack's body?" Kirsten

"Look at that, Kirsten!" Lars said.
"Look at all those pelts! And all of them the finest fur!"

said. "I wish Papa were here to tell us what to do!"

"Papa always knows what's right," Lars said. He took off his woolen cap and scratched his head, then he bit his lower lip. "Kirsten, do you know what I think Papa would tell us?"

"What, Lars?"

"He'd say that we have to bury Old Jack, that's what," Lars said.

"But we *can't* bury Old Jack," Kirsten said. "We can't dig him a grave while the ground is frozen."

"Then we'll have to come back and bury him in the spring," Lars said. "Papa would never leave a body unburied, I know that." He paced back and forth as he thought. "Do you know what else Papa would tell us?"

Kirsten shook her head.

"Papa would say that if Old Jack doesn't have kin, then his things belong to whoever finds them. And we found them."

Kirsten plopped down on the little three-legged stool by the fire hole. "Do you mean they're ours like finders-keepers?"

"No, it's not like finders-keepers. If Old Jack were alive and we found something he'd lost, we would give it back to him. But he's dead and gone, so we can't give him back these furs. We can't give him anything but a proper burial. He doesn't even have a family to do that."

Kirsten looked again at Old Jack, then at the big stack of furs. "Are you sure Papa would say Old Jack's things are ours?" she asked.

"I'm sure!" Lars said.

"Even all his furs?" Kirsten asked again.

"Even his furs," Lars said firmly.

"Oh, Lars," Kirsten breathed. "Those furs are worth a lot of money!"

"That's what I'm thinking, Kirsten. And I'm thinking how much we need money now. Old Jack's furs might even be worth enough to buy the Stewarts' house."

Kirsten rested her chin on her hands. She wanted to be glad about the furs, but she felt tears brim at her eyes. "Lars, it's a dark night with no moon. Even with a lantern, I don't know if we can find our way home. And it's bitter cold! How will we ever take so many furs with us?"

Lars was piling up kindling and split wood. He

lit the fire and knelt beside her. "Don't cry, Kirsten. I have a plan. Just listen to me."

Kirsten scrubbed at her cheeks. Lars could always make a plan, she thought. If she had to be lost in the woods, she was glad she was with her big brother!

"First," Lars said, "it's much too dangerous to try to get home in the dark. Second, we're safe here from the cold and from wolves. So we have to stay until it's light. Third, in the morning we'll load the pelts onto our toboggan and follow the stream home."

Still Kirsten was troubled. "But what about Old Jack? We have to bury him! Especially if we're going to take his furs."

"Of course we'll do right by Old Jack," Lars said. "For now we'll cover him with a blanket. In the morning, before we leave, we'll pile stones against his door so animals can't get in. When Papa comes back in the spring, the ground will be thawed. Papa and I will dig Old Jack a grave. We'll bury him, and Papa will say the burying prayers."

Kirsten rocked back and forth on the little stool. "Lars, it's a good plan. But I don't want to stay the whole night in this cave with a dead man!"

When Lars folded his arms he looked just like Papa delivering a lecture. "Old Jack was a good man and his soul is in heaven. There's nothing to be scared of."

He set a thick log on the fire. "Now we've got to get some rest. I'll keep watch, and you lie down on that blanket and sleep."

Kirsten shivered, but she did as Lars said. She lay down on the blanket and drew her knees up under her chin. She closed her eyes tightly and tried to sleep. But she was as wide awake as if morning had come already.

"Lars?" she whispered.

"Are you thinking about Old Jack?" Lars said.

"I'm thinking how scared Mama will be when we don't come home tonight," Kirsten said.

"Mama knows we can find shelter," Lars said. "Remember, once you and Papa hid in a cave during a snowstorm. Go to sleep now."

Kirsten didn't think she would sleep. How *could* she? But when she opened her eyes, a line of morning light showed around the door. An Indian blanket covered Old Jack's body. Potatoes roasted in the coals of the fire. And Lars was already tying the furs into bundles to load onto the toboggan.

"Get yourself up!" Lars cried. "We've got to take these furs home to Mama!"

CHAPTER
FIVE

WELCOME HOME

Soon March rains began to melt the deep snow. When the ice on the streams thawed, the trapping season was over. But with Old Jack's pelts and the ones from the trap line, the Larsons had enough money to buy the Stewarts' house. Papa wrote that he and Mr. Stewart had shaken hands on the deal. "Make our new house ready," the letter said. "I'll be home in April!"

Mr. Stewart was the first one to come back from the logging camp. Soon after he arrived, the Stewarts loaded up their things and set off to join the wagon train for Oregon. The next day, the Larsons got ready to move into their new house.

Everyone helped. Anna folded clean diapers on the bed where Britta played with her rattle. Lisbeth and Kirsten packed sweaters and shawls into the blue trunk. Lars carried out the traps, and Peter stacked wood for the stove into the wagon. Aunt Inger and Mama packed flour and salt and coffee and other things for cooking into a wooden box.

"Here's an extra skillet," Aunt Inger said. "Take it along. And here's a stew pot I don't often use."

"You've given us so much already," Mama said. "You mustn't give us your pots and pans, too."

But Aunt Inger put the pot into the box. "How will you feed the children without a pan to cook in? Did the Stewarts leave any plates behind?"

"They said they would leave some plates and spoons and cups," Mama said. "They even left some of their furniture, and straw mattresses and a few blankets, too. A covered wagon doesn't hold very much."

Aunt Inger put her fists into her waist and smiled at the small pile of the Larsons' belongings. "You could put everything here into a covered wagon and still have lots of room left over!"

Mama sank down at the table and sighed. "If the Stewarts hadn't left behind their table, Papa would have to build one for us before we could have supper."

"Where is Papa?" Kirsten said. "Mr. Stewart came home more than a week ago. He said Papa and Uncle Olav would come on the next boat."

"Papa will be here as soon as he can," Mama said. "I want to have our new house clean and shining for him. I want him to walk in and find us all just as he left us last winter."

"He'll find that Britta's grown twice as big!" Aunt Inger said. She gave the baby a kiss on top of her blond head, and then another kiss to Anna.

Anna made a little moan like the sound of wind under the door. "Ohhh! It will be so lonely without all of you sharing the farm with us!" she said.

Kirsten felt lonely, too, the way she'd felt when she waved good-bye to Mary and John and their family. She sat down on the bed beside Anna and took her hand. "We're going to live just a few miles away, Anna. We'll see each other often."

Anna put her head on Kirsten's shoulder. "I'll

miss talking at bedtime. Can I sleep at your house someday?"

"Of course you can," Kirsten said. "I'll be alone in the trundle bed until Britta outgrows her cradle."

Mama put her hands on Kirsten's and Anna's knees. "There's no reason for those long faces, girls. Today we're moving into our new house, and before long Papa will be with us again."

But Kirsten saw that Mama blinked tears, too. Happy times could bring tears just like sad times.

Aunt Inger pulled a soft old carpetbag from under the bed and scooped the clean diapers into it. "We won't put this carpetbag into the trunk. You'll need these diapers before you need anything else. Now let's get your things into the wagon," Aunt Inger said. "Lisbeth and Anna and I will come along later with a big pot of soup for your first supper in your new home!"

Kirsten had run up the lane to the Stewarts' house many, many times. But today, as Lars drove

their wagon up the lane, the house looked new and special and full of surprises, like a gift. *This is our house,* Kirsten whispered to herself. Every night from now on her family would sleep under that wide shingled roof. Every morning they would walk out that door onto their very own land.

Peter jumped out of the wagon even before Lars reined in the horse. Caro bounded out right at Peter's heels and scampered to the door, barking as if he knew he belonged here now. Britta smiled and bounced in Mama's lap as though she'd like to run, too. Kirsten tied Blackie to the hitching post, and Mama climbed down out of the wagon.

"Open the door, Kirsten," Mama said. "Peter, you carry Britta so she doesn't get in the way and get hurt. We'll take the trunk inside first."

Kirsten opened the front door and peered inside. She had been in this house so often she knew it almost as well as Aunt Inger's house. But without John and Mary here, the house seemed quiet and empty. "Hello?" Kirsten called, and the echo greeted her, "Hello!"

"I didn't realize how heavy this trunk is!" Mama said.
"How did you manage to pull it out of the fire all by yourself, Kirsten?"

The door opened into the big kitchen. Peter carried Britta inside. Then Lars dragged the trunk into the doorway, and Mama and Kirsten came behind to push it over the sill.

"I didn't realize how heavy this trunk is!" Mama said. "How did you manage to pull it out of the fire all by yourself, Kirsten?"

"I was so frightened I was strong," Kirsten said.

"And there weren't so many things packed in the trunk then," Peter said. "I bet I could have saved the trunk, too!"

"You saved the baby, Peter!" Kirsten said.

"This trunk came all the way from Sweden," Lars said. "Now it's got to come just a little farther. Push one more time!"

He yanked and they shoved. The trunk scraped through the door, and suddenly Kirsten and Mama were inside the house, too.

Sunlight shone through the glass window as though a hundred candles lit the room. The house smelled of the bread Mrs. Stewart had baked for her family's journey to Oregon, and of lye soap. Peter set Britta down on the scrubbed floor. She crawled to the table and pulled herself up and laughed, as though she announced, "Here we are!"

Mama spread her arms wide and gazed around the kitchen as though she saw it for the very first time. "Look how big it is!" she said. "And we have a fine cook-stove, and cupboards for our dishes! And a chest for our clothes! And shelves, too, lots of them!"

"We have a wood floor like the one at Aunt Inger's!" Lars said.

"And we have a good strong table," Mama said, "and even chairs!" Mama stroked the back of one. "When we sit at our table, we can look out the window and see that big maple tree." She sighed. "Oh, this is a real home, isn't it! This is the home your papa and I dreamed we'd have in America."

Peter dashed into the next room. "We have two big beds and a trundle bed, too!"

Kirsten followed Peter. There was another glass window in this room. She had spent many happy hours with Mary on the bench under the window. Here they'd practiced their reading and made up stories. Here they'd played with their paper dolls

and told secrets and made promises. Kirsten knelt on the bench. This would be a good place for her and Lisbeth and Anna to work on their quilting, she thought.

Kirsten put her fingertips on the cool windowpane. She could see the rope swing in the maple tree. She and Peter would love that swing! When Britta was older, they'd swing her in it, too. And under the maple was a nice patch of shade where Mama could do her mending on hot summer days. It would be good to live in this house.

A bit of paper tucked into the corner of the

window frame caught her eye. She pulled the paper free and unfolded it.

The note was in Mary's pretty handwriting.

Dear Kirsten,
Please be happy in your new house. The next time I write it will be from Oregon! Don't forget your loving friends,
Mary and John
P.S. John made the little toy for you!

Kirsten looked carefully at the little toy. On one side was a picture of a bird cage. On the other side, a bluebird. When Kirsten spun the toy, the bird seemed to fly into the cage. There it was, safe and happy, like Kirsten in her new home. The secret good-bye from Mary and John made her heart even lighter, like a bird fluttering under her ribs. She put the letter and the toy into her pocket. Her friends wouldn't forget her, and she would never forget them, not ever!

Then a figure came into view far down the

road. Kirsten pressed her forehead against the windowpane to see better. A man was walking in long strides. Could it be Papa? Yes, it was Papa! He was back from the logging camp at last. And he was just in time to be with them in their new house!

"Mama!" Kirsten called. "Papa's back! Here he comes right now!" She ran into the kitchen and opened the door.

Peter skidded out through the door with Lars right behind him. Mama hurried with the baby hugged to her shoulder. "Welcome home! Welcome home, Papa!" Kirsten called as they all hurried to the gate to meet him.

A Peek Into the Past

CHANGES FOR AMERICA

A painting of Saint Paul, Minnesota, in 1855.

As Kirsten grew up, more and more people traveled west across America to start new farms. New settlers moved closer to one another, and farm villages turned into bustling little towns with churches, schools, and town halls. There were more stores because there were more farmers with more things to buy and sell. Families started to plan weekly trips to town, not only to shop but also to visit with friends. They held socials and dances and church suppers so that neighbors could meet. The lonely times of the Larson family's first years on the frontier were over.

Farms weren't isolated from the rest of America,

Farm families liked to get together for dances and dinners.

Trains carried the mail across America.

either. The railroad, that "iron horse" that carried Kirsten and her family to the edge of the frontier, was linking cities and farms across the country. By the time Kirsten was twenty-four years old, the first *transcontinental railroad* in the world joined America from coast to coast.

Because of railroads, farm families didn't have to make everything they needed the way pioneers did. They could buy things directly from stores in faraway cities. Farmers would study a store's newspaper ads, then mail an order and money to the store. Trains delivered the mail, and the store sent out the things the farmer had ordered on the next train. By the time Kirsten was a young woman, this kind of shopping started a new industry—the mail-order business. Today, people still shop from mail-order catalogues, except now they call on the telephone and their orders are brought

Railroads also carried the things people ordered from catalogues.

Godey's Lady's Book showed American women the latest fashions.

to them by trucks and airplanes as well as trains. Of course, there were no trucks or airplanes when Kirsten was growing up.

Trains also carried ideas to America's farms. Farm girls and women read about the latest fashions in magazines that came to them by train. And families waited eagerly for the train to bring the next part or *installment* of the popular stories that were published in monthly magazines. There weren't radios or televisions for news and entertainment back then.

Trains also brought new farm equipment. As Kirsten grew up, factories were making stronger plows and machines like threshers and reapers. These machines helped farmers produce much more food than their families could ever eat.

Big machines made men's farm work easier.

Farm families could sell their extra crops.

So farmers sent their extra crops back to towns and cities where they could be processed and sold. Farms like the one Kirsten lived on became "the nation's breadbasket," feeding people who lived throughout America.

Farms also got bigger and bigger, until they were too big for a family to work alone. When Kirsten married, she and her family would not have worked together in the fields the way the Larson family did. Instead, Kirsten's children would go to school and her husband would work the land with the help of *hired hands,* or farm helpers.

Although new machines and hired hands made a farmer's work easier, women's work on farms didn't change much during Kirsten's lifetime. As a farm wife, she would work from sunup to sundown, cooking and cleaning for her big family and the hired hands. She would milk cows,

Even when Kirsten grew up, women's work on farms was hard.

A modern kitchen like this still didn't have running water.

take care of the chickens, sell eggs, churn butter, and keep a large garden so there would be plenty of food to preserve for winter.

Some modern equipment made Kirsten's life easier than Mama's had been. Kirsten probably cooked on a brand new cast-iron range that had an oven in it. But she still had to lug wood into the house to keep the stove full, a job that was just as heavy and hard for her as it had been for Mama. Kirsten probably had a pump outside in the yard so she wouldn't have to carry water from the stream. But doing the laundry was still an all-day chore. She would pump water into a bucket, heat it on the stove, scrub the soiled clothes against a metal board in a washtub, hang them out to dry on a clothesline, then press them with a heavy iron she heated on the stove. In the evenings, Kirsten would mend and

THE PATENT CLOTHES DRYER.

Heavy "sad irons" had to be heated on the stove.

Kirsten's sewing machine was powered by her feet, not electricity.

sew clothes for her large family, but a modern sewing machine made this chore easier than it had been for Mama. If she were lucky, Kirsten would get a pump in her kitchen by the time she was forty years old. But she would never have had electricity, running water, or an indoor toilet in her farm home.

Although work on the farm continued to be hard, most American families chose to live on farms throughout the 1800s. People liked life on the farm because they enjoyed working together as families on land that had belonged to their parents. After all, a chance to own land of their own was the main reason that families like the Larsons had come to America in the first place, and people like Kirsten and her children were proud to keep that tradition alive.

THE AMERICAN GIRLS COLLECTION

There are more books in The American Girls Collection. They're filled with the adventures that three lively American girls—Kirsten, Samantha, and Molly—lived long ago. You'll want to read all of these books to see how growing up as a girl in America has changed and how it has stayed the same.

But the books are only part of The American Girls Collection—only the beginning. There are lovable dolls—Kirsten, Samantha, and Molly dolls—that have beautiful clothes and lots of wonderful accessories to go with them. They make these stories of the past come alive today for American girls like you.

MOLLY
SAMANTHA
KIRSTEN

To learn about The American Girls Collection, fill out this postcard and mail it to Pleasant Company. We will send you a newsletter with more interesting things to read about Kirsten, Samantha, and Molly, and a catalogue about all the books, dolls, dresses and other delights in The American Girls Collection.

- -

I'm an American girl who loves to get mail. Please send me:

□ The **catalogue** of The American Girls Collection

□ The **newsletter** of The American Girls Collection (published in March and September)

My name is ______________________________

My address is ______________________________

City ______________ State ______________ Zip __________

My Birthday is ______________________ My age is _____

I am in ___ grade. Parent's Signature ______________________

The book this postcard is in came from: □ a bookstore □ a library □ a friend/relative □ the Pleasant Company Catalogue

If the postcard has already been removed from this book, and you would like the Pleasant Company newsletter and catalogue, please send your name and address to:

PLEASANT COMPANY
P.O. Box 497
Middleton, WI 53562-9940

NO POSTAGE
NECESSARY
IF MAILED
IN THE
UNITED STATES

BUSINESS REPLY MAIL

FIRST CLASS PERMIT NO. 1137 MIDDLETON, WI USA

POSTAGE WILL BE PAID BY ADDRESSEE

PLEASANT COMPANY
P.O. Box 497
Middleton, WI 53562-9940